The Wimbols of Wombledon and the Magic Wishing Tree

Wayne Morgan

© 2020 Wayne Morgan. All rights reserved.

No part of this book may be reproduced, stored in a retrieval system, or transmitted by any means without the written permission of the author.

AuthorHouse™ UK
1663 Liberty Drive
Bloomington, IN 47403 USA
www.authorhouse.co.uk
Phone: 0800 047 8203 (Domestic TFN)
+44 1908 723714 (International)

Because of the dynamic nature of the Internet, any web addresses or links contained in this book may have changed since publication and may no longer be valid. The views expressed in this work are solely those of the author and do not necessarily reflect the views of the publisher, and the publisher hereby disclaims any responsibility for them.

Any people depicted in stock imagery provided by Getty Images are models, and such images are being used for illustrative purposes only.
Certain stock imagery © Getty Images.

This book is printed on acid-free paper.

ISBN: 978-1-7283-5197-1 (sc)
ISBN: 978-1-7283-5198-8 (e)

Print information available on the last page.

Published by AuthorHouse 04/06/2020

The Wimbols of Wombledon

And the Magic Wishing tree

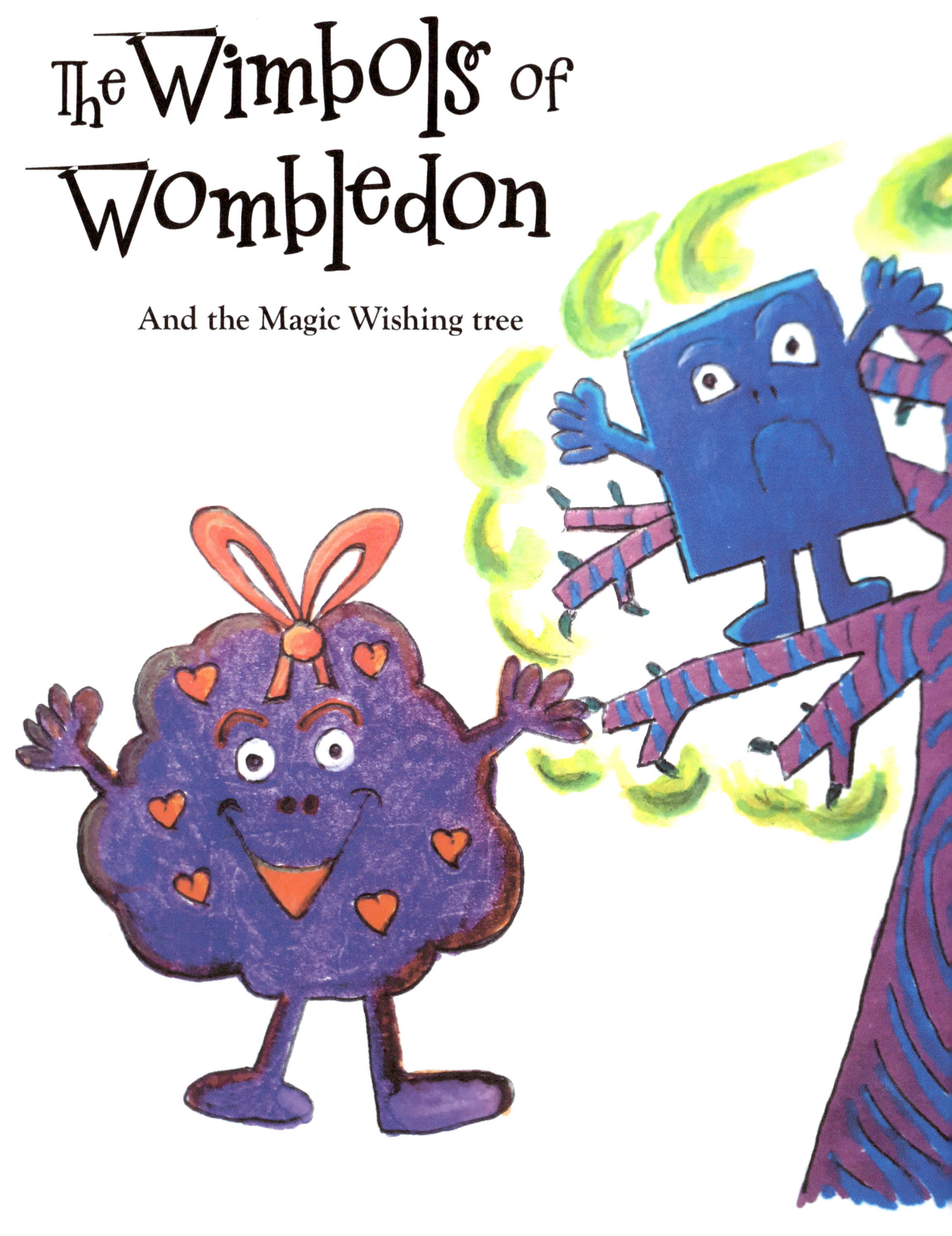

To my beautiful girls.
~~~~~~~~~~~~~~~~~

Sam

Anwen

Talisee

Love always

Wayne

The Wimbols of Wombledon
are happy and free,
with smiles on their faces
as big as can be.

They like to laugh,
Joke and play

and some of the misgogs
would even say
They're the happiest souls,
on the earth to this day.

They have no worries,
They have no strife,
They just smile
And get on with life.

The misgogs are happiest when theres someone to blame

So not very often that such a shame!

The misgogs arn't happy you see
They moan all the time,
Why's that not me!?

They're always smiling
its just not fair!

I want to be happy!
but I just dont dare!

The misgogs want to be
happy you see
with their downward
Smiles stuck up in a tree

To live life down on the ground, Not up in our tree.

I want to be happy and smile.

To be happy and smile for the whole world to see

Hey you misgogs, come down
from your tree!

Come sing and dance with us,
Smile and just be!

Were happy, unhappy,
Just let us be.

Just leave us here,
up in our tree.

But they weren't really happy but they wanted to be.

So slowly, one by one,
they climbed down from
their tree.

They thought there's no harm
to just look and see.

For they lived in a magical wishing tree.

They had their eyes closed
So they didn't see.

They imagined a thing,
and it would just be.

You imagine life hard
and it was.
No reason, just because.

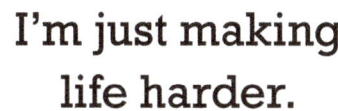

I'm just making
life harder.

For no reason!

you made a monster
to scare you at night,

You made him real scarey
to give you a fright.

Now imagine, loves in everything
everything you see,
every bird and every tree.

even you and even me.

Now dream the dream
of happiness.
and life is if you dare!

You could live life happy
and live without a care.

Smile each day,
that comes your way,
and then all of the others.

Thank you, for your smile

Thank you for yours.

Then just take that smile,
and share it with
your sisters and your brothers.

This may not work everyday
but at least its worth a try.

Coz its better to laugh & smile
Than just to moan and cry.

The misgogs are happy now
Im sure that you will find

They spend most days smileing,
are friendlier and kind.

Now everybody loves them
and they're fun to have around

Way up in their tree
or even on the ground.

And with less time
Spent moaning
theres more time now for fun,

We have more time now for fun.

Theres more time now
for everything,

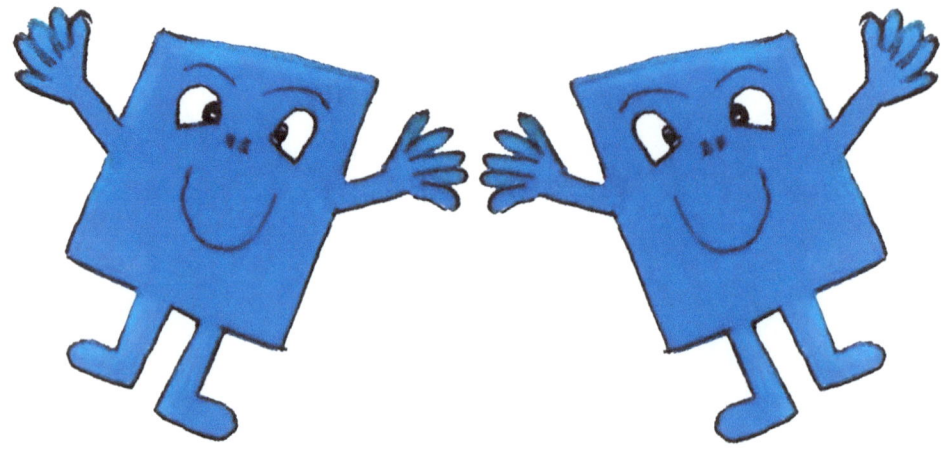

the stories just begun.